MW00981368

Dreams do come true.

Iris Campbell

IVAN AND THE MAGIC RAINBOW

By
IRIS CAMPBELL

ILLUSTRATED BY
ERICA DISSLER

© Copyright 2006 Iris Campbell.
All rights reserved. No part of this publication may be reproduced, stored in a retrieval system, or transmitted, in any form or by any means, electronic, mechanical, photocopying, recording, or otherwise, without the written prior permission of the author.

Note for Librarians: A cataloguing record for this book is available from Library and Archives Canada at www.collectionscanada.ca/amicus/index-e.html
ISBN 1-4120-8798-8

Printed in Victoria, BC, Canada. Printed on paper with minimum 30% recycled fibre. Trafford's print shop runs on "green energy" from solar, wind and other environmentally-friendly power sources.

TRAFFORD
PUBLISHING™

Offices in Canada, USA, Ireland and UK

Book sales for North America and international:
Trafford Publishing, 6E–2333 Government St.,
Victoria, BC V8T 4P4 CANADA
phone 250 383 6864 (toll-free 1 888 232 4444)
fax 250 383 6804; email to orders@trafford.com
Book sales in Europe:
Trafford Publishing (UK) Limited, 9 Park End Street, 2nd Floor
Oxford, UK OX1 1HH UNITED KINGDOM
phone +44 (0)1865 722 113 (local rate 0845 230 9601)
facsimile +44 (0)1865 722 868; info.uk@trafford.com
Order online at:
trafford.com/06-0554

10   9   8   7   6   5   4   3   2

A SPECIAL thanks to my husband, Colin for his patience and encouragement. My thanks to the following: Ben Smit (Boltzap wouldn't be the same without you!); Kari Campbell-Headley, who was my personal editor. Last but not least, my granddaughter Lauren, her teacher Mrs. Buckley and the grade three class in Denver, CO for doing a test run – thank you for your thumbs up!

IVAN AND THE MAGIC RAINBOW

IVAN LEAPT up, his head colliding with a cross-beam. "Ouch!" he moaned, rubbing an instant goose egg. When did he fall asleep? He shook the hay from his mop of thick brown hair and peered over the edge of the loft.

"Good, you're still here," he whispered.

He ran back to the house, his bare feet skipping over chicken poop on the way. He grabbed the phone and punched buttons.

"Jake? It's me. Come over real fast, I have something incredible to show you."

With a pencil wedged sideways in his teeth, Ivan grabbed his journal and went back outside. He flinched when the screen door slammed behind him.

"Ivan Tippen! What did I tell you about slamming that door?" called his mother.

"Sorry, Mom," said Ivan, spitting out the pencil. He pursed his lips and let out a whistle. "Come on, Kody, let's go." The Great Pyrenees bounded across the grass, the raccoon mask circling his eyes gave the huge dog a somber look.

Ivan decided not to do his daily routine; he wanted to get back to the barn. He set the journal down on the rickety board that half-covered the empty rain barrel. His morning always started with checking the weathervane for the direction of the wind and recording the temperature on the big round thermometer mounted on the side of the barn. Below it hung the barometer. He checked that too. He dreamed of being the best weatherman in Morristown, or even the whole world!

"What's up?" Jake hollered, stirring up a cloud of dust with his bike.

"I heard noises coming from the barn last night," Ivan said. "They sounded like a zillion little bells. At first I thought my ears were ringing. I snuck out of the house to check it out. It was real scary 'cause it was thundering and Kody was no help – he hid in the closet! After what I saw in the barn, I'm glad he wasn't there."

"What did you find?" asked Jake.

"Follow me!" said Ivan.

The barn was dark and eerily quiet; the air

reeked of musty, stale hay. Ivan aimed his flashlight on the ladder leading up to the loft.

"We have to climb up there first," he whispered.

"Are you sure it's safe?" Jake asked. His green eyes began to blink like the signal light on his grandpa's old tractor. Ivan knew Jake too well; when his friends eyelids started to flap, Jake was getting nervous.

"Don't be such a worrywart, Jake."

The ladder groaned from the weight of the two boys. They stepped off the top rung and flopped onto a bed of hay.

"Over here," said Ivan, crawling on his belly to the corner of the loft.

"What is it?" asked Jake. He turned his ball cap backwards and followed. Ivan stopped, stuck his nose in the air and sniffed.

"It's just sour manure," said Jake.

"Nope, I smell rain," said Ivan.

"Would you stop it, you're not a weather-man!"

"Grandpa can smell rain, and so can I," Ivan grumbled, and moved closer to the edge.

A flash of lightning lit up the barn.

"Five-ten-fifteen – "

"Now what?" Jake asked.

KA-BOOM!

Thunder crashed overhead drowning out Jake's voice.

"I was counting to see how many miles away the thunder is," said Ivan. "Did you know sound goes about 1,000 feet per second?"

"Look, Lightning-head show me what's so in-credible."

"Okay, okay, don't get so excited," said Ivan, pointing his finger. "Down there in the corner, see?"

"Wow!" said Jake. His eyes bugged out and his mouth gaped open.

A faint glow lit up the corner of the barn. The boys stared wide-eyed at seven strange creatures huddled together. They looked like humungous snails, the size of one of those giant pumpkins at the Fall Fair. The glow was a different color for each shell, and the tips of their foot-long tubular antennae were lit up like miniature flashlights. Between each antenna were large aqua-green eyeballs the size of golf balls. A nose obviously wasn't an option, since there wasn't one.

"What are they?" Jake asked, his voice sounding shaky.

"They're konkles," Ivan whispered. "Dad read me a story about them a long time ago. No one knows why, but they always travel in groups of seven. During bad storms they find a warm place to hide. Isn't it cool that they found our barn?"

"No kidding!" said Jake. "I've never heard of a konkle before."

"The book says they've out-lived dinosaurs. Do you think your grandpa would know about them? He was a weatherman once," said Ivan.

"Let's call him," said Jake.

Down the ladder they scurried.

In less than an hour the boys ran and opened the gate for Grandpa Windsor. He bounced around like a ping-pong ball in the worn seat of the old John Deere tractor. Pulling up next to the barn, Grandpa shut off the engine. It coughed and sputtered and finally died. Grandpa eased himself to the ground.

"What's the weather forecast for today, Ivan?" he asked and gave him a wink.

Ivan felt his face redden. Nobody took him seriously about his weather predictions.

Ivan's Dad stopped spreading the manure and shook Grandpa Windsor's hand. "We need rain and lots of it. Not even our young weatherman here can foresee that happening anytime soon."

"You have to see this," said Ivan. He pulled up his sagging blue jeans and led them into the barn.

"Hokey-Dinah! Would you look at those?" said Grandpa Windsor in his raspy voice.

"Can I keep them, Dad?" asked Ivan.

"According to an old weatherman in Wannabey, konkles survive on earth only for a short period of time," said Jake's grandpa, scratching his wiry gray beard. "If I remember correctly, they have something to do with rainbows."

"Really? Our grade four class is studying rainbows," said Ivan. "Dad, can I stay out here tonight and keep watch?"

"I don't know. It might be dangerous."

"Can I stay too? Please Grandpa?" said Jake.

Grandpa Windsor looked at Ivan's dad, arched one bushy eyebrow and chuckled. "It's okay with me, but Mr. Tippen has the final say."

"I suppose; but this had better have a positive effect on your homework project," said Mr. Tippen.

"Thanks, Dad!

"Thanks, Mr. Tippen. Thank you, Grandpa!" said Jake.

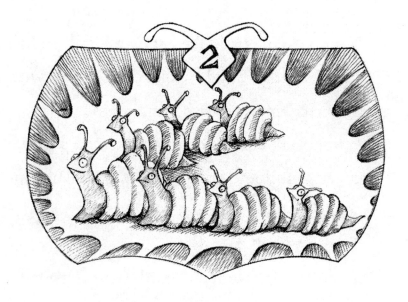

MRS. TIPPEN prepared a snack and dragged out an old blanket, all the while lecturing the boys on what to do and what not to do in a barn at night.

Ivan rolled his eyes recalling her comment yesterday on his bedroom; convinced his mother's expertise was on pigsties. He left Jake to listen to the drill and went in search of the book on konkles.

Afraid of frightening the konkles Ivan and Jake tiptoed back into the barn. Ivan tossed the old wool blanket over the hay. They tried desperately not to make a sound while trying to smooth out the blanket. Unsuccessful they soon gave up. The straw won the battle, poking and jabbing them through the blanket.

Jake settled down on his side of the bed, tore open a bag of corn chips and began munching.

"BURP!" his hand flew over his mouth; his eyes bulged when he looked at Ivan.

"Sshh!" said Ivan, with a scowl. He opened the tattered and dog-eared book and scoured each page in search of information. Flipping to the last chapter Ivan grinned like a Cheshire cat. "Here it is, 'The Transformation of the Konkle.'"

Jake exhaled a massive yawn.

"It is believed the konkles leave immediately after the storm is over, and always in the direction the storm left in. When the sun appears the transformation begins. The konkles turn, face the sun, and one by one they change into one of the colors of the rainbow." Ivan glanced over at Jake. "This is going to be amazing!"

Jake was sound asleep.

Ivan was too excited to sleep. He crept down the ladder and cautiously approached the konkles.

"Hi," he whispered. "My name is Ivan. I won't hurt you; I just want to know more about you."

The konkles immediately moved into a V-formation, like geese do when they fly south. The one in the front made a motion with his head and its antennae bobbed up and down. It was asking Ivan to come closer, he was sure of it!

"I'll move real slow; please don't be frightened," said Ivan, his heart racing.

The same konkle bent his head forward. The tinkle of bells echoed softly in the barn; again, its head bobbed up and down. Ivan reached out with his hand and inched closer. The konkle rested one of its antennae in Ivan's clammy palm.

"Wow," Ivan whispered. "A funny vibration is going through my body."

"That's because I have joined our electrical paths."

"You can talk!" Ivan froze, his jaw dropped as if the hinge had snapped. His hands tingled. His hair stood on end, as if it had been rubbed with a balloon. He saw his shadow on the wall – he looked like Frankenstein!

The deep mechanical voice spoke each word slowly and precisely. "We can only communicate when you hold my antenna."

"Do you have a name?" asked Ivan.

"My name is Randu. I am the red refractor of the rainbow and the fastest." His large fluorescent eyelids blinked slowly as he spoke. "The other konkles form an arch beneath me in their own refractor colors."

"You must have magical powers, otherwise how could you be a konkle one minute and a rainbow the next?" asked Ivan.

"Our magical powers are limited to the transformation process. The true magnitude of our power can only be used against Boltzap," he replied.

"Who is Boltzap?" asked Ivan, his curiosity mounting.

"Boltzap is the Cloudiferous Ruler of storms. A danger and a menace to the universe," said Randu.

"How can you stop him? He sounds powerful and scary! How do you change into a rainbow?" asked Ivan. "I'm studying rainbows in school. This would be unbelievable for my project. No one in my class will top this story!"

"You ask too many questions."

Ivan brought his face down closer examining Randu's antenna, still feeling the strange vibrations tingling through his body. He was curious how or what made it glow. It looked like Jell-O gelatin but it didn't jiggle or squish between his fingers. It was solid but not hard and felt warm in his hand.

"What are you doing?" asked Randu.

"I-I-um, I was wondering if I could have magical powers to control the weather. Only in a good way, honest!" Ivan quickly added.

"It may be possible. For what reason should this power be granted to you?"

"I overheard Mom and Dad talking last night. Dad said we're going to lose the farm to the bank if this drought continues. Dry lightning and thunder is making it worse. All I want to do is make things better."

"Hmm, I will have to assemble the konkles

on the new moon. The decision must be unanimous for the magic powers to be granted," said Randu.

"Great, the new moon is tomorrow night. Dad says we don't have much time left and the forecast is for more hot weather," said Ivan.

"Meet us back here at this same time tomorrow for the answer."

Ivan said goodnight to the konkles and climbed the ladder to join Jake. Sleep was the farthest thing from his mind. He tucked his arms behind his head and listened to Jake purr like an old tomcat.

Blink, the red-tailed rooster crowed loudly into the morning air. Ivan bolted up, missing the crossbeam by a hair. He elbowed Jake in the ribs.

"Wake up, sleepyhead. It's time to get up," said Ivan.

"Are the konkles still here?" asked Jake, his eyes still closed.

Ivan peered over the edge of the loft. "Yep. Wait until you hear what happened last night!"

Jake listened wide-eyed as Ivan told him of his encounter with the konkles.

"You sure it wasn't a dream, Ivan? Nobody's going to believe a konkle can talk!"

"Trust me, Jake, this was no dream. Tonight's the new moon and that's when they'll decide if I can have magic powers," said Ivan, following Jake down the ladder. "We had better not tell anyone, it would be too risky. The konkles would be captured and maybe destroyed."

"You're right about that part. Our parents would freak out. I have to admit, I'm a bit freaked out myself," said Jake.

"Me too!" said Ivan. "Let's check out the weather forecast."

"Race you to the house," said Jake.

"You're on!" said Ivan, and shot past him.

The boys laughed and shouted pushing and shoving each other through the kitchen door. The screen door slammed shut behind them.

"Oops! Sorry, Mom," said Ivan, giving her a hug.

Kody pressed his wet nose against the screen door and let out loud 'woof'.

The airwaves crackled with static as Ivan turned the dial on the radio to the local weather station. Thunderstorms were still in the forecast, that meant the konkles wouldn't be leaving to-day.

Since the konkles appeared to feel safe hiding in the barn, the boys were allowed to stay out another night. Ivan was anxious to hear what the konkles had decided.

IVAN AND Jake watched nervously as the konkles slowly moved into their V-formation.

At long last Randu bobbed his antennae. Ivan stepped forward and reached out his hand. Randu rested one antenna in Ivan's palm. "A stranger is with you. Can he be trusted?"

"Don't worry. Jake's my best friend," said Ivan. "Have you decided?"

"We have," said Randu.

The tension mounted; the only sound in the barn was the wind whistling through the cracks.

"Do I get the magic powers?" Ivan asked, his voice a hoarse whisper.

"You shall hear the answer now," said Randu. He turned and faced the konkles. "May I have the vote please, Wazzu?"

Wazzu, the smallest refractor, moved beside Randu and bobbed his antennae up and down.

Ivan reached out his other hand and Wazzu rested a small antenna in it.

"It is a unanimous 'yes,' said Wazzu, his voice a much higher pitch than Randu's. "Randu will instruct you."

"You must obey all the signals of the magic antenna and memorize the magic words," said Randu. "Most important, this power bestowed upon you must be used for prosperity, NOT devastation. I shall grant you only three magic commands, therefore you must use them wisely. Should you choose otherwise, the consequences shall be enormous. Do you understand, and promise to obey these rules?"

"I promise," said Ivan.

"Then let us begin."

Jake nudged Ivan. "I'm scared, aren't you?"

"A little, but I trust Randu. I don't think he would harm us."

A scraping sound behind them made the boys turn around. The konkles were slowly inching their way toward the barn door.

"The time has come for us to leave. The storm is over," said Randu. "Ivan, first you must stand with your back to the sun and face the rain. Do NOT look back under any circumstances. Second, take hold of my antenna and do not let go, no matter what happens."

"I understand," said Ivan, feeling dizzy from excitement.

"Then we are ready," said Randu.

A multicolored trail of slime was the only evidence left in the barn of the konkles visit.

Ivan held onto Randu's antenna as he was told.

"What if something goes wrong? Maybe I should get Grandpa, this is getting too weird," said Jake, following so closely Ivan could feel him breathing down his neck.

"Nothing will go wrong. There you go worrying again."

Spectacular rays of sunlight penetrated through the drifting clouds. A fine mist of rain fell, forming a veil over the farm. A few miles away large thunderclouds held the mountaintops hostage with the possible threat of yet another storm.

"Are you ready, Ivan?" asked Randu, bobbing his antenna up and down.

Ivan was having difficulty holding on. "I am, but you're bobbing too fast. Slow down, okay?"

"Do not let go, and do not look behind you!"

A burst of green and blue sparkles cascaded down around the boys. Randu had just regenerated a new antenna for the one Ivan held in his hand!

Ivan blinked, thinking his eyes were playing tricks on him. He rubbed his eyes with one hand and struggled to hold onto the antenna with the other hand.

"Did you see that?"

"Wow!" said Jake.

They watched Randu and the other konkles fade. It was slow at first then the transformation sped up. Ivan and Jake stared in awe at the empty space where only a moment ago the konkles had been.

Ivan's trance was broken when Jake yelled. "Look – over the barn!"

A rainbow, the biggest one Ivan had ever seen arched over the horizon. Violet, indigo, blue, green, yellow, orange and red colored the sky in a majestic halo.

"They did it, they did it! We actually witnessed the transformation," said Ivan. "Now is my chance to try out the magic antenna. Dad will be flabbergasted when I change the drought over the past two years into the perfect growing season. We'll have the best crop of potatoes in the world," said Ivan. He grinned a mischievous grin.

"Do you remember all the magic words?" asked Jake. "What if you make a mistake, and change us into giant snails or worse, into girls?"

"Quit being a pain. I have everything under control, and yes, I remember all the magic words!"

Ivan cupped a hand over his eyes, squinting into the sun. Slowly he scanned the farm. It was like a desert, the soil dusty and lifeless. The rows of potatoes normally hilled at this time, drooped in despair from the heat. The small amount of rain from the last two nights had evaporated as quickly as it had fallen.

The loud racket of hundreds of crickets kicking up their own storm filled the air.

"Remember the teacher telling us how to tell the temperature by the crickets? How did that go again?"

"Who cares? Are you doing the magic spell or not?"

"I got it! You have to count the number of chirps in 15 seconds, multiply by four and you've got the temperature in Fahrenheit," said Ivan.

"Whoopee," said Jake, in a sarcastic tone.

Ivan was silent for a moment, listening. "It's

ninety-six degrees!" He shouted.

"Which cricket did you listen to?" Jake asked, rolling his eyes.

They looked at each other and burst out laughing.

Ivan continued his surveillance of the farm. Near the barn he saw his younger sister Miranda studying something in the grass.

"Jake, I bet Miranda has found another prize bug," said Ivan.

"Hey, Ivan! Look, I found a brown speckled spider for my collection," shouted Miranda, waving a butterfly net in the air.

"Way to go, Sis," said Ivan. "Told you, Jake." He knew Miranda wasn't your normal six-year-old. She loved collecting bugs more than anything.

Ivan cleared his throat and hoisted up his pants. "Ahem. Attention everyone and everything within the sound of my voice," he called out across the field. "I'm about to brew up a weather special never seen before. Rain to water the crops, followed by warm sunshine to bud the spuds. Morristown will have record-breaking crops. With one wave of my magic antenna and, of course the magic words, we shall prosper like never before!"

"Ivan, you're not Merlin the Magician so cut the abracadabra stuff. Besides, you're acting weird and scaring me. Maybe I should get Grandpa in case something goes wrong."

Ivan ignored Jake and with both hands he tightened his grip on the magic antenna. He slowly began to chant.

Rain, I do call –
Rain, you must fall –
From a cloud you will pour –
Until the earth is dry no more.

The words were barely out of Ivan's mouth

when a loud rumble sounded behind him.

He turned around almost dropping the magic antenna. A gust of wind appeared out of nowhere, whirling and twirling around him. It gained more speed and dragged large black thunder boomers in its wake.

"Ivan, you were supposed to ask for rain, not a storm! Those clouds mean trouble," said Jake.

Another rumble sounded, louder this time, and more cumulous storm clouds approached overhead. Daylight vanished into near darkness. Splatters of rain, the size of pellets bounced knee-high off the ground. The black ominous clouds crashed together with a deafening boom.

Ivan looked up and came face to face with a black, ferocious, billowing cloud. He couldn't believe his eyes; the cloud had bulging bloodshot eyes and a nose that resembled a head of cauliflower. The sneer on its crooked mouth sent a shiver down Ivan's spine.

"Let's get out of here!" said Jake.

IVAN STOOD stunned, frozen in place. "Did you see that cloud? It's Boltzap! Randu warned me about him. I must've used the wrong magic words!" said Ivan. "I have to stop him before he makes the storm worse." He lifted the magic antenna into position. It vibrated faster and faster. He fought to keep his grip.

"Jake, help! I can't hold onto this thing, it's too

powerful."

A fork of lightning flashed across the sky, lighting up Boltzap's face. It looked like a skull from the grave!

"Let's get out of here! Miranda's still out in the field! Lightning could strike her," said Jake.

"I need your help NOW, Jake! Miranda's okay; she'll run back to the house. Just get over here." Ivan shouted. He couldn't believe he was ignoring the plight of his sister.

Jake hurried to Ivan's side and gripped his pudgy fists around the antenna next to Ivan's.

"Listen carefully. I'm going to try Randu's other command, so don't let go!" The vibration made his cheeks jiggle as he spoke.

Another flash of lightning lit up the sky.

Ivan began his chant.

Rain, I do call –

Rain, you must fall –

From the sky you will pour

Until the earth is dry no more.

"That's it, Jake! I used the word CLOUD the first time. That's what brought Boltzap."

Another crash of thunder directly above them made the boys drop to their knees and cover their ears. Ivan tucked the antenna beneath his trembling body.

Rain spat from his sneering mouth as Boltzap roared, "It's too late, my friend. You have brought me back from years of non-precipitous boredom. I am, thanks to you, the Cloudiferous Ruler again!"

"Ivan, I'm definitely going to get Grandpa. We need his help!"

"No, I can handle this. I have the power!"

Jake was already running toward home as if

he were doing the 100-yard dash for money.

Ivan looked up at Boltzap trying hard to conceal his fear. He raised the antenna and pointed it. "I have the power to destroy you!"

"Release Randu's magic antenna, I am in control now."

"Ivan, help me!" called Miranda.

Ivan turned and saw his sister sobbing uncontrollably in the open field. Her denim patched overalls hung wet from her small frame. She looked so frightened and kept calling his name. He had to decide whether to run to Miranda or keep Boltzap from taking the antenna.

"Release the magic antenna or I shall destroy all that is around you," Boltzap roared.

"Never!" Ivan shouted.

Boltzap inhaled deep enough to suck in Ivan and a small barn. His evil eye sockets sparked a jagged bolt of lightning. It danced across the field

– straight for Miranda!

"Miranda! Miranda! Drop to your knees and don't let your head touch the ground," yelled Ivan. He remembered reading those instructions in his book on lightning. What on earth was taking Jake and Grandpa Windsor so long!

He heard a familiar bark behind him. Kody bounded through the high grass toward Miranda. He must have heard her call for help. Kody pounced high into the air and landed on Miranda as if she were a field mouse. He covered her with his massive white furry body as another flash of lightning reached them. Ivan heard a loud whimper – then silence.

Ivan swallowed hard.

"This is only a sample of what is to come. Surrender the magic antenna," roared Boltzap.

"No way!" shouted Ivan. He figured he had three choices and time was running out. He could surrender to Boltzap and have the earth suffer in the hands of this evil windbag. His next choice would be to save Miranda and Kody or his last choice – risk using the last magic command and hope it worked.

"I need help, big time," Ivan moaned and searched the sky. "Randu, can you hear me?"

A wrinkled hand grabbed Ivan's shoulder from behind, startling him. Ivan whirled around and faced the angry glare of Grandpa Windsor. Grandpa Windsor grabbed hold of the magic antenna.

"What are you doing? Trying to destroy everything with your one-man magic show?" he wheezed, out of breath from running.

"Something went wrong, I guess," said Ivan, staring down at his dirty shoes.

"I should say so, young man."

"Miranda and Kody –?"

"Jake's checking on them now."

"I still have one more chance," said Ivan.

"You want one last chance to ruin our crops forever!?"

"This is all your fault!" Ivan shouted. "You couldn't remember the important stuff about konkles. I hope I don't get old like you! A grandpa is supposed to be crammed full of history, that's why they live so long!"

The old man turned and started walking away.

"Where are you going? Aren't you going to help me?" shouted Ivan.

Grandpa Windsor kept walking, his tattered flannel coat tails flapping in the wind.

A sharp pain penetrated Ivan's skull, and his eye sockets began to throb. He felt dizzy. "Grandpa Windsor, please come back. I don't know why I said those things; I didn't mean it. Please, I need you!" Tears welled up in his eyes. Something was happening to him; he felt his knees buckle, and he slumped down onto the grass.

"Grandpa, Ivan fell!" said Jake as he ran with Miranda and Kody toward Grandpa Windsor.

"Ivan, what's wrong?" shouted Miranda, wiping her tear-stained face.

Grandpa Windsor turned and ran back to where Ivan lay.

He propped Ivan up and rested him in the crook of this arm. He patted Ivan's face and gently shook him. Ivan groaned. "You came back."

"What happened?" asked Grandpa Windsor.

"I-I don't know. My head hurts, and my eyeballs feel the size of basketballs. Miranda and Kody, are they okay?"

"I'm good, and so are my bugs," said Miranda. She proudly held up the net for him to see.

"The lightning hit a rake next to Kody," said Jake.

"Boy that was lucky! I'm sure glad I forgot to put it away yesterday."

"You best be taking Miranda and Kody back to the house where they will be safe, Jake," said Grandpa Windsor.

"Okay, but I'll be right back."

Ivan watched Jake head toward the house with one hand clutching Miranda's and his other hand holding Kody's collar. Kody kept glancing back struggling to free himself.

Boltzap's billowing mass hovered over Ivan. "Now will you surrender the magic antenna? This is your last chance, or you will slowly change into a konkle."

"Use the last magic spell, Ivan. It's our only chance," said Grandpa Windsor.

"I'm not sure I remember it," said Ivan.

"Aha! It may be too late, it is only a matter of time and your body will begin to change!" said

Boltzap, a sneering grin stretched across his ugly face.

"Grandpa Windsor, what are we going to do?" Ivan asked, scratching his chest. Something was on his skin – he lifted his shirt. A shell-like substance was growing on him! The buttons on his shirt stretched to the breaking point.

"Help, look at me!" said Ivan, his voice sounded different, and the tinkling of bells sounded when he moved. "What's happening to me?"

"HA, HA, Ha! This is marvelous, absolutely brilliant!" laughed Boltzap.

Ivan felt his head getting heavy as he glanced up at the darkened sky. Boltzap, surrounded by more taunting, black, thunderous clouds loomed overhead with a menacing grin. The wind played havoc with the tall grass whipping it back and forth, around and around in a frenzy. It blew so hard the grass was whistling an eerie tune as it thrashed about.

"Why am I getting so sleepy?" asked Ivan.

"I'm not sure, but you have to try and remember the last magic spell! Look at you, soon you'll be a konkle and there will be no going back. Unless –" said Grandpa Windsor. He stroked his beard deep in thought.

"Unless what?"

"Unless you're able to summon the konkles back," he said.

"Randu made me promise to use the spells wisely and I have failed him. What if he refuses to come to my rescue? I will end up a konkle or worse, a lone refractor – useless! I may as well be dead," said Ivan, wiping his eyes with his shirt-sleeve.

"Well, we can sit here and feel sorry for ourselves, or try to solve the problem. What shall we do?"

"I'll summon Randu," said Ivan, staggering to his feet. "Besides, the pain in my head is getting worse, and this itching is driving me crazy!"

"Look at the horizon at those crepuscular rays. No wonder after the dust, then the thunderstorm and all that moisture. Mighty pretty, but it also means it will be getting dark soon," said Grandpa Windsor.

"Maybe Boltzap has given up getting the magic antenna. It's awfully quiet," said Ivan, looking down at his shirt. Two buttons were missing.

"Here comes Jake. Maybe he can help you remember the spell," said Grandpa.

Jake leapt through the tall grass, frantically waving his arms in the air. Ivan saw Jake's mouth moving, but the wind grabbed his words and tossed them away.

"There's another storm coming, worse than

the first one," said Jake. He rested his hands on his knees, puffing and panting. "The weather station says it's due over Morristown in about three hours."

"Do you know what that means?" asked Ivan. "The konkles will come back and hide in our barn like last time."

"That's not for certain. You still have to remember the spell, and the sooner the better," said Grandpa.

"You forgot the last –?" Jake stopped in mid-sentence. His mouth gaped open in disbelief. "What's that on your forehead?"

"What do you mean?" Ivan asked. He touched his forehead with his hand. "Oh, my g...!" the words faded away, he felt the color drain from his face.

Another button flew off Ivan's shirt when he bent to pick up the antenna. Jake stared in horror at Ivan's scaly skin.

"Look at you; you're turning into a konkle! What's going to happen to you? Now I know I wasn't scared for nothing," shouted Jake. "Boltzap is just waiting for the right moment. Guess what, Mr. Weatherman, we'll be lucky if Morristown survives his evil storm!"

"That's enough, Jake. We have to get Randu to return, or Ivan has to remember the spell, and fast," said Grandpa.

"I can't believe you forgot it! You said you remembered them all," said Jake, his eyes blinking faster and faster.

"Thanks for nothing, friend! Why don't you take your sissy and sorry butt home!"

"Fine, I'm outa here," said Jake. He turned and ran without looking back.

"Well, well, I figured you had enough problems, but I guess one more won't hurt," said Grandpa.

He lifted his hat and scratched his balding head.

Ivan watched Jake disappear around the side of the barn. "He's supposed to be my friend. What kind of friend wimps out in a crisis?"

"Jake's reacting like any friend would. He's scared for you and that's his way of showing it. We're running out of time, you had best concentrate on remembering the spell. You can worry about Jake later."

Ivan slumped to the ground, exhausted. His head pounded; he felt the two bumps on his forehead growing larger. The last button shot off his shirt like a missile, landing somewhere in the grass.

A rumble of thunder sounded in the distance. The wind churned the tall grass, tossing it back and forth in a dizzying flurry. Clouds slid quickly across the sky, building into dark monstrous thunderheads.

"Try using the last spell to summon the kon-kles. The downside is, we're at the mercy of Boltzap if it doesn't bring them back. Didn't you say Randu would return if you ran into trouble?" asked Grandpa.

"Yes, but I'm scared what he will do," said Ivan.

"It can't be any worse than what Boltzap will do, right?"

"I guess so. Can you help me up?"

Grandpa secured his long arms under Ivan's armpits and hoisted him to his feet. Ivan staggered about until Grandpa took hold of him by the scruff of the neck for balance.

"You okay?" asked Grandpa.

"No, but I have no choice," said Ivan. He raised the antenna, looked up at the sky and closed his eyes.

Randu, I do call -
All konkles large and small –
To my rescue, I truly need
The spell to abolish Boltzap's deed.

Grandpa lowered Ivan to the ground and let him rest his head on his lap. "Was that your last spell?"

"No, I still have a third and final one. That spell was what Randu said to use if I absolutely needed him. I sure hope it works or I've really messed up."

Grandpa and Ivan scanned the sky looking for signs of Randu or worse, Boltzap. Both were lost in their own thoughts. The clouds loomed overhead bumping into each other and created more rumbling. Flashes of lightning zipped across the distant sky heading their way.

"Nothing is happening," said Ivan. "Except for

me. My arms are now starting to itch. I'm scared."
He put his face in his hands and released a flood
of tears.

Grandpa stood up and rubbed his aching back.
He nudged Ivan and pointed toward the east.
"Look!"

"What, where?" Ivan asked, wiping his eyes.
He reached for Grandpa's hand, unsure of his
balance. Ivan couldn't believe what was before
them.

THE UNDENIABLE tinkling of bells resounded in the wind. An array of tiny flickering lights only seen in the Milky Way or the Northern Lights floated across the horizon from the east. The wave of lights approached faster, wafting through the sky like a stingray gliding through the ocean.

Ivan felt different. The itching stopped and so did the excruciating pain in his head. Fearful, he reached with a trembling hand and touched his forehead.

"Grandpa, they're gone!" he shouted. "The antennae are gone! Look, even the scales are disappearing!"

"It appears your urgent call to Randu has been answered," said Grandpa Windsor. They exchanged a high five.

Ivan jumped when a bolt of lightning spliced through the clouds.

"This is your last chance!" roared Boltzap. "Surrender the magic antenna now and the storm will end."

"Look!" said Ivan, pointing at the hideous face of Boltzap.

"I have an idea that just might work," said Grandpa. "But it's going to require a great deal from you."

"What can I possibly do without Randu's help?"

asked Ivan. "I don't understand what's taking them so long. They should be here by now."

"Remember the electrical charge that enabled you to communicate with Randu? We are going to use the same process – but in reverse."

"Huh?" asked Ivan.

"You've read enough on thunder and lightning storms," said Grandpa. "Do you remember about the development of a thundercloud? Positive and negative electrical charges are carried to the cloud. Now I want you to think of Boltzap as a giant storage battery. As he moves along, the positive charges follow like a shadow. Air is a poor conductor – not like trees, buildings or people. So, when Boltzap reaches his potential of about a billion volts, the insulating air can no longer resist. This is when he releases a giant spark. What you have to do while holding onto the antenna, is aim it at the spark then zap it before it reaches the ground."

"But, don't I have fifty milliseconds before the dart leaders begin to flash?"

"That's right, but this is our only chance."

"I'm not so sure about this," said Ivan.

"You have to try."

"Okay, but will this help bring the konkles back?" asked Ivan.

"We can only hope," said Grandpa.

Boltzap inflated himself larger than before; more black evil clouds buffered up next to him for added strength. The wind howled like a lone coyote in the desert.

Ivan attempted in vain to clutch his button-less shirt. The menacing wind ripped it from his grip. He felt as if he would be airborne any minute. Rain drops the size of marbles pounded against his skin. Fighting the wind he grasped the antenna with both hands and held it as high as he could. It wobbled back and forth from the force of Boltzap's power.

"HA, HA, HA!" said Boltzap, his laugh ugly and sinister. "You cannot go up against me, the Ruler of Storms. Your time has come. Say good-bye to the magic antenna!"

"Not on your life you big fog head! Your time has come," said Ivan. He mustered enough courage to keep his voice from shaking.

Grandpa Windsor stood close by. This was Ivan's moment of glory or – doom.

Boltzap scrunched his cauliflower nose and inhaled, nearly pulling himself inside out. The wrath of Boltzap's anger charged the air with an electrifying current. The blast of wind from his cavernous mouth sent Ivan stumbling backward. He gripped the antenna using every muscle in his body.

Grandpa moved behind him. "He's getting

ready, Ivan. The next lightning flash ejected from those eye sockets is the one you have to connect with. You have the power right there in your hands."

"No pressure. Right?" said Ivan. He wondered if Grandpa could hear the fear in his voice.

Boltzap with his cavalry of ornery black clouds whirled into position. They circled Ivan like a cowboy's lariat. He leapt out of the way avoiding a shingle from the barn roof that shot past him. Mini wind tunnels spun around like tops. Ivan had a hard time seeing.

The earth appeared to stop rotating on its axis; the air froze in an electrical haze. Darkness engulfed them. The only glimmer of light came from the magic antenna.

"The antenna, Grandpa – look, it's working!" shouted Ivan. "The magic spell, I remember it now!"

"Do you know what that means? You have doubled our chances of getting through this," said Grandpa, his bottom lip quivering anxiously.

Ivan nodded his head; his whole body shivered. He closed his eyes tight and made a promise that he would give up television for an entire month if he could pull this off.

"Are you ready?" asked Grandpa.

"I – I think so," said Ivan, struggling to hold the magic antenna steady. He looked up and his eyes targeted on the grotesque face of Boltzap. He knew there was no turning back. It was now or never.

BOLTZAP REARED his enormous, black diffused vapor into position. He appeared ready to make his move. The wind was stronger than ever, howling and whirling around their heads, taunting them.

"Get ready, Ivan. Your time has come," said Grandpa, holding onto his hat.

Ivan took one last look eastward in hopes of

seeing Randu and the konkles. The wind drowned out any hope of hearing the tinkling of bells. Dark clouds hovered over them like an unwanted blanket on a hot summer's night. He looked over at Grandpa Windsor and took a deep breath.

Boltzap snarled. "Look around you. This farm will never be the same again. I shall destroy it all. Prepare yourself – Boltzap rules again! HA, HA, HA!"

Startled, Ivan jerked his body around allowing the magic antenna to slip through his hands. He grasped the end of the antenna milliseconds before it would have hit the ground. Boltzap began emitting a low rumble.

"Hold the antenna higher," shouted Grandpa. "You have to be ready!"

"I know, but it's getting heavy, and Boltzap spooked me."

"That's part of his plan," shouted Grandpa.

The air became electrified; Ivan felt the static electricity swarming around them. Boltzap tested the air with a flicker of lightning. Ivan's scalp tingled. His hair stood on end. Tightening his grip, he planted both feet firmly apart for balance – he was ready!

The next flash came directly into the path of the magic antenna. Ivan took aim and began to chant.

Heed me, Boltzap for you shall die -
A spell surrounds you in the sky-
Cloudiferous Ruler never more -
Your power lost just like before.

The sky exploded into a fireworks display of red, yellow, green and blue. A sonic thunder boom followed each flash of lightning. Boltzap's rage amplified. He spat out hailstones the size of golf balls.

The magic antenna was in control. Jagged flames of red, and orange spewed high into the clouds. A meltdown of vapor changed the hail to rain, pounding the ground with a vengeance. Boltzap released an agonizing groan. Then – total silence. The wind and rain stopped as if a tap had been turned off. A loud swishing sound and the tinkling of bells replaced the seconds of deathly quiet.

Soaked to the skin, Ivan wiped the rain from his face using Grandpa Windsor's shirt-tail. "Look. It's Randu!"

"You did it – you brought them back! The spell worked." He put his arm around Ivan and gave him a squeeze.

A magnificent rainbow formed before their eyes. Ivan hugged the magic antenna close to his chest. The bells became louder and closer. He looked around but saw no sign of the konkles anywhere.

"Look over there," said Grandpa, pointing toward a fading rainbow.

"It's disappearing. But why? Where's Randu?" asked Ivan.

The tinkling of bells resounded behind them. Ivan whirled around, his eyes lit up at the sight of the konkles. Randu bobbed his antennae and Ivan quickly responded by taking one in his hand.

"I have come for the magic antenna," said Randu. "You failed to keep your word. Place it on the ground before you."

"Randu, I didn't do it on purpose. I don't know why or what happened. Everything went out of control after the first spell. How was I to know Boltzap would appear?"

"Place the magic antenna at your feet," said Randu.

"But – but, you must believe me. I only wanted

to be the best weatherman in the world and bring rain for our crops. I didn't plan a disaster," said Ivan.

Randu and the other konkles moved in closer.

"Please, Randu, you have to forgive me. Give me one more chance and I promise nothing like this will happen again," said Ivan, taking a step back.

"It is too late. You can never be trusted again. Put down the antenna. You remember the consequences," said Randu.

Ivan's chin dropped, tears welled up in his eyes. He slowly bent down and rested the magic antenna at his feet.

A thin blue laser shot from the end of Randu's tail, striking it. The antenna melted into a gooey blob of jelly. The konkles disappeared.

Ivan dropped to his knees onto the wet grass. He gently placed his hand on the transparent puddle. "I'm so sorry."

Grandpa Windsor tapped him on the shoulder. "Come on, let's go home. I think you have some homework to do."

IVAN SHOVED open the window of the loft and stared out. The sun cast its warm rays upon him. It made him feel toasty warm on the outside, but not on the inside. He was having difficulty concentrating on his project for school. The events over the past few days played over and over in his mind. How could he make up to Miranda for deserting her when she needed him the most?

Jake's silent treatment gnawed at him. He realized now how much he missed his best friend. He had to find a way to get things back to the way they use to be. Ivan reflected on how badly he had treated Jake's Grandpa.

His mom and dad were more than a little upset with him. He was grounded from watching television for two months. That's like a life sentence without parole!

"Yep, I sure messed up good," said Ivan, out loud to no one.

Gathering up his scattered homework he shoved it into his backpack. He crawled over to the edge of the loft hoping to see Randu and the konkles again. This had all started with them. He could almost see the seven creatures huddled together in the corner of the barn. Their slimy trails were barely visible now.

"Ivan?" A soft whisper came out of nowhere.

Ivan nearly jumped out of his skin. He stuck his head over the top rung and peered down into the dark shadows of the barn. "Miranda, is that you?"

"Yes. Can I come up?" she asked.

"Be careful and don't look down, okay?" said Ivan.

Miranda climbed the ladder successfully. She jumped onto the bed of hay with a huge grin on her freckled face.

"Aren't you still angry with me?" asked Ivan.

"Nope. Never in a zillion years could I stay mad at you," said Miranda. She crawled over to her brother and gave him a big hug.

"Yikes, Miranda, don't let my friends see you do that!" said Ivan, he gave her a wink and hugged her back.

In an attempt to make up to his sister he filled her in on all the details with the konkles. Miranda stared wide-eyed, hanging onto every word.

"Wow," said Miranda.

"Pretty hairy, don't you think?" He looked at his watch. "I have to go now, kiddo. I've got things to do."

Ivan coached Miranda down the creaky ladder, slowly, one rung at a time. She jumped from the last one and shouted, "Ta da!"

"Go and play with your bugs now, okay? I'm off to Jake's house."

He watched her skip back to the house singing 'Itsy Bitsy Spider.'

"One down-four to go," said Ivan.

He jumped on his mountain bike and headed down the dirt path.

Hesitating, Ivan suspended his knuckles in mid-air before knocking on the door. Butterflies danced the tango in his stomach. The rickety old porch creaked and groaned as if feeling his agony. He took a deep breath and rapped on the door. The knock was louder than he had intended. He nervously smacked his baseball in and out of his worn-out glove, and waited.

The door opened wide and Grandpa Windsor's large frame filled the doorway. He peered over the top of his glasses. "Well, look who's here?"

"Hi, Grandpa Windsor, may I come in?" asked Ivan.

"You betcha! Jake, Ivan is here to see you."

"Actually, I came to see you too," said Ivan. "I don't think I thanked you properly for helping me with Boltzap. I said awful and rude things to you. I want you to know I didn't mean any of it. I hope you will forgive me, sir."

"I appreciate your coming here on your own steam to apologize. It takes courage to admit when one is wrong. Apology accepted, young man. Now, let's see what's keeping Jake."

"Thanks, Grandpa Windsor," said Ivan, and smiled to himself as the old man slowly meandered down the hall in search of Jake. "Two down – three to go."

Jake sauntered into the cluttered foyer giving one of his gumboots a kick out of the way. Ivan felt Jake's eyes blazing through him. His body released a nervous shudder.

"Hi," said Ivan. It sounded more like a croak.

"Hi," said Jake, his eyes piercing through him.

"Want to play catch?" asked Ivan.

"I don't know. Maybe," said Jake.

Grandpa Windsor placed a hand on a shoulder of each boy. "I think tossing that ball back and forth may be the best thing. It'll burn off some of that tension. Friendship is worth the effort, don't you think?"

Ivan and Jake looked at Grandpa Windsor and then at each other for what seemed an eternity.

"I'll get my glove," said Jake. He turned and ran out of the room.

"Thanks," said Ivan, with a big smile.

Jake threw the ball with an energy Ivan hadn't seen before. He actually fell on his butt from one throw and then missed it by a country mile.

"Hey, what are you trying to do?" asked Ivan.

"Who's the sissy now, Mr. Weatherman?"

"Aw, come on. You know I wasn't serious. I was taking my frustration out on you. Isn't that what friends do, then they get over it – right?"

Jake aimed the ball at the puddle of water at his friend's feet. It hit the target, splattering Ivan's pants with mud.

"Okay, I deserved that. I'm really sorry about what happened. Can't we be best friends again?"

asked Ivan. He walked over to Jake and gave him a friendly push nearly knocking him over.

"Watch it!" said Jake. "You want to know what really hurts?"

"I got a feeling you're going to tell me," said Ivan.

"You're right. I am. You never let me help with Boltzap or with the konkles. It was just you and Grandpa. How would you feel being left out?" asked Jake.

"Yeah but, Jake you were scared, remember? All you wanted to do was to go home and hide under the bed. What kind of help is that?"

"Well, someone had to be afraid. And I wasn't under the bed! You were acting weird, and besides someone had to look after Miranda. You sure weren't," said Jake.

"Okay, we're even. I'm sorry, and thanks for looking after my sister."

"Me too, and you're welcome," said Jake.

"Want to work on our homework project?" asked Ivan. He crossed his fingers behind his back.

"I suppose," said Jake. He gave Ivan a gentle push. The two boys chased each other, laughing back to the barn.

"Three down – two to go," said Ivan to himself.

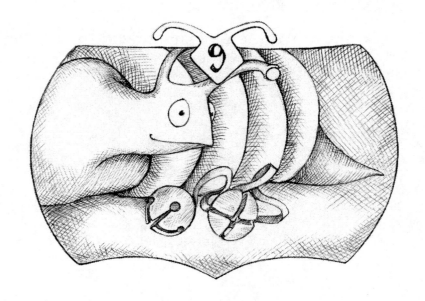

"DID YOU hear that?" asked Ivan, sitting up straight.

"Hear what?" asked Jake. "I didn't hear anything."

Ivan moved to the edge of the loft and looked down. "Hand me the flashlight. I know I heard something."

Jake rummaged through the scattered papers

and found the flashlight poking out of the hay. Ivan flashed the beam of light onto the floor below.

"What are we looking for?" he asked, in a whisper.

"Over there," said Ivan, pointing to his right. "I can't believe it!" He doused the light and clamored down the ladder at record speed.

"Wazzu, where did you come from?" asked Ivan. "Where are Randu and the others?"

Jake moved next to Ivan. Wazzu looked up at the two boys with glazed eyeballs. They reminded Ivan of doughnut tidbits, only with a black dot in the center. Wazzu bobbed his miniature antennae slowly up and down. Ivan knelt down and cupped his hand around one of them.

"Hello, Ivan," said Wazzu, his voice barely audible.

"What happened? Why are you here alone?"

asked Ivan.

Jake edged closer and crouched down beside them.

Wazzu moved his eyeballs from one boy to the other. "I lost my refractor when we rescued you from Boltzap. Without it I am unable to rejoin the others." A tiny tear slid down his leathery face.

"Can we help find it?" asked Jake.

"Yeah, together we'll find it. All you have to do is tell us what to do," said Ivan.

"Without my refractor, I am unable to send signals to Randu. My communicator was also destroyed," said Wazzu.

"You mean that tinkling bell sound? Is that your communicator?" asked Ivan.

"Yes. Without it I am doomed."

"I have an idea. Why can't we imitate the sound of bells? We have jingle bells packed away in our Christmas stuff," said Ivan.

Wazzu's small round face lit up. "Do they really sound like our bells?" He asked. "It is most important that they resonate as close to ours as possible."

"Let's find out. Come on, Jake, let's look in the storage room," said Ivan.

"Stay here, Wazzu. We'll be right back," said Jake.

The boys scrimmaged through all the boxes that were marked in black felt pen, CHRISTMAS DECORATIONS.

"Don't break anything or Mom will ground me for life," said Ivan.

"I found them!" said Jake. His head surfaced from a huge box. Silver and gold tinsel dangled from his hair. The bells jingled as he freed them from the tangled tree lights.

"Great! Let's get back to Wazzu and see if they'll work," said Ivan.

They scurried back to the barn. Wazzu was right where they had left him. He looked up with hope in his eyes.

Ivan reached into his pocket and pulled out the tiny bells. Wazzu's eyes brightened. He began bobbing his antennae repeatedly. Ivan gently shook the bells.

"Here, Jake. You hold the bells while I take Wazzu's antenna so he can speak to us," said Ivan.

"What do you think, Wazzu?" asked Ivan.

Jake wiggled and jiggled the bells.

"It might work. Can we try now?" asked Wazzu.

"You bet!" said Ivan.

"I must be in exactly the same place as when we first arrived. Most important, I have to rest on Randu's refractor trail. This will provide the best transmitter effect," said Wazzu. He moved ever so slowly toward the corner of the barn.

"I'm sure glad there is some of it left," said Ivan.

Wazzu got into position. "This is my only chance. If it works, Randu will restore my refractor and transmitter."

"Should we ring the bells now?" asked Jake.

"I'm ready," said Wazzu. He pulled his antenna from Ivan's hand and closed his eyes.

The bells tinkled in the quiet, musty air of the barn. Ivan and Jake took turns ringing them. They watched and listened.

'WOOF!' The boys jumped. Wazzu pulled his head in close to his body. His eyes bugged out even more than normal.

"Kody, what are you doing in here? Come on, boy, let's go see Miranda," said Ivan. Taking Kody by the collar he escorted him out of the barn.

Ivan re-entered the barn and stopped dead in

his tracks. A soft glow of lights lit up the corner where Wazzu was huddled. He ran over to Jake, who stood like petrified wood with his mouth agape. His only movement was his hand slowly jingling the bells.

"You okay, Jake?" said Ivan, in a whisper.

"I-I don't know," said Jake, without blinking.

"Stop with the bells for a sec, Jake. Listen," said Ivan, cocking his head to one side.

Barely clearing their heads, a swirl of coloured lights swayed down and around them. The ghostly lights danced to the music of the tinkling bells.

"Egad, what was that?" said Jake.

Before Ivan could answer Randu appeared before them. One by one the other konkles lit down beside him.

"Randu, you're back!" said Ivan.

Randu bobbed his head motioning Ivan to approach him and hold his antenna.

"I can't tell you how happy I am to see you again," said Ivan.

"You have earned our trust again, Ivan. You found a way to help Wazzu in his time of need. That is most honorable. Our rainbow will once again be complete, thanks to you," said Randu.

"Jake helped too," said Ivan, tugging on Jake's sleeve to move closer.

"Our thanks to him as well," said Randu.

"We have to finish our school project for tomorrow morning, and – well – I was wondering if you would be able to help us out," said Ivan.

"What exactly do you want from us?" asked Randu.

"I haven't quite finished putting my idea together yet. Can I tell you in the morning? Would you stay in the barn tonight? Please?"

"That would be most unusual, considering it is not a stormy night," said Randu.

"But we could, couldn't we?" asked Wazzu. He nestled up to Randu so Ivan could hold his antenna too.

"Your request has been granted," said Randu. He signaled the konkles to move into the V-formation. "We shall be here for you in the morning."

Ivan and Jake beamed at each other and scurried up the ladder to put the finishing touches on the plan.

"Four down – one to go!" said Ivan in a whisper only he could hear.

MONDAY MORNING was a flurry of activity. The teacher helped the children rearrange the room for extra seating. Their parents were the special guests for the project presentations.

Laughter and squeals of excitement echoed off the high ceiling of the large room. The metal folding chairs clattered and banged against each other as they were unfolded and set into place. The blackboard was erased of the last lesson, filling the air with chalk dust. Each student's rainbow masterpiece proudly decorated the walls around the room.

The teacher, Miss Myrtle, tapped her pointer on the desk for everyone's attention.

"Our guests will be arriving shortly. Please take your seats and I will read out the order of presentations."

Ivan and Jake slid into their seats as if they were home plate.

"Are you nervous?" asked Jake, in a whisper.

"A bit," said Ivan. "I sure hope our plan works."

Miss Myrtle stood before the class; she looked more like a librarian than a teacher. Her graying hair was tied neatly back in an old fashioned bun. The plain black dress she wore was cinched tightly at the waist and hung down below her knees. Her brightly polished black shoes appeared snug on her feet causing her stockings to wrinkle like an elephants knees. She tapped on the desk and the classroom fell silent. All eyes focused on their teacher.

"Today is the day we have all been waiting for," said Miss Myrtle. "I will read the names out at random and that will be the order of presentation. Your parents should be arriving shortly and I expect you to be on your best behavior." She rattled off the names on her list with quick precision.

Whispers buzzed throughout the classroom when she finished. A knock on the door silenced everyone. All heads followed Miss Myrtle as she opened the door and greeted each parent, including Grandpa Windsor. The shuffle of chairs and secret waves to parents sent the room into a flurry of giggles and whispers.

"We would like to thank the parents for attending our rainbow presentations," said Miss Myrtle. She slid her spectacles down from the top of her head and picked up the papers. She nodded at the first student to begin.

The students were each given five minutes to do their presentation.

It seemed forever before it was Ivan's turn. Thank goodness there were only twelve students in the class, he thought. The butterflies in his stomach were back and his knees felt like putty. Ivan repeatedly glanced out the window and over at Jake.

"I feel like I'm going to throw up," said Ivan.

"You'll do fine. Quit worrying, you're beginning to sound like me," said Jake, with a grin.

"The final student to present his project is Ivan Tippen," said Miss Myrtle.

Startled, Ivan jumped up so quickly the papers

slipped from his hands and scattered at his feet.

"Sorry, Miss Myrtle," said Ivan, he felt his face redden all the way back to his ears. He bent down and gathered the papers as quickly as he could. The class burst into giggles until the teacher called for silence.

Ivan walked up to the front of the class, the papers vibrating in his hand. He took one last look out the window, and then at Jake.

"Ahem. The storm we had over Morristown last week was a rare and majestic one. I would like to share with everyone the part I played in that storm. The rainbow is much more than what we actually see it as. It's made up of real aliens. Each alien is a refractor color of the rainbow. There are thunder clouds that are evil destroyers of the earth."

"Excuse me, Ivan," interrupted Miss Myrtle. "This project was to be based on fact not fiction, dear." She was clearly distraught as to where Ivan's story was leading.

"Please, Miss Myrtle, let me finish. Everything I am about to tell is the truth and really happened," said Ivan.

The classroom erupted in begging and pleading for Ivan to continue.

Jake stretched his arm above his head and waved it high into the air to get the teachers attention.

"Yes, Jake?" asked Miss Myrtle. "What is it?"

"I'm a witness to Ivan's story. Please, can he finish?" asked Jake.

"Well, this had better prove to be based on fact, Ivan or you will get a failing grade," said Miss Myrtle. "You may continue." She sat down and nervously surveyed the parents as if trying to read their minds.

"There is more to a rainbow than what we

read in books," said Ivan. "My presentation will reveal the unbelievable and incredible history of this magical prism in the sky."

The tension in the room could have been cut with a knife. All eyes were on Ivan as he moved across the room. He opened the first window, then the next and continued down the room until all six windows were open. Spits of rain splattered his notes. The cumulus clouds lingered in the sky overhead. According to Ivan's plan everything was a go.

He walked over to the whiteboard, picked up a marker and began drawing a thundercloud. The marker seemed to have a mind of its own, emphasizing the ugly cauliflower face of Boltzap. His hand became a blur as he sketched and filled in the details, complete with huge raindrops plummeting to earth.

Ivan turned to his audience. "This is the cumulonimbus cloud known as Boltzap. He is the Ruler of Storms and was released from his years of darkness by a magical antenna granted to me by the largest refractor of the rainbow, Randu. Seven konkles form a prism of light; each one generating its own refractor color and together they arch over the sky to form a rainbow."

The audience was captivated, even the adults were glued to their seats in anticipation.

"I can prove to you now that rainbows are a magical phenomena. I am going to end my presentation with the help of my alien friends, and my human friend, Jake Windsor."

Right on cue, Jake scrambled from his seat and joined Ivan at the open windows. They reached into their pockets and took out the jingle bells. The tiny silver bells dangled from a piece of colored ribbon and sparkled and twinkled under the ceiling lights.

Ivan jiggled his hand, starting the bells jingling. Jake joined in with his. Watching out the window, it took less than a minute and they cupped their hands around the bells to silence them.

"Listen," said Ivan.

The boys turned and faced everyone. Ivan held a finger to his lips. "Shhh!"

The room fell silent. Ivan watched his classmates on the edge of their seats.

The tinkling of bells rode in on a soft breeze through the open windows, over the heads of the stunned audience and back out again. Ivan pointed out the window. Everyone gasped at the sight of seven konkles only yards away on the grassy slope of the playground. The largest of the konkles, Randu down to Wazzu the smallest. Randu looked back at Wazzu. They nodded their antennae at each other. Right before the bug-eyed classroom, they dissolved into a haloed prism of the seven spectacular colors of the rainbow!

"Wow!" said the audience in unison.

Miss Myrtle approached the front of the class. She seemed to be having difficulty speaking. She kept trying to clear her throat.

"Ivan, that was a splendid and such an unusual approach to the research of rainbows. The class will now vote on the winner of the Rainbow Project Award. Use the ballet handed out earlier, and write the name of your winner," said Miss Myrtle.

All heads went down. The only sound was the scratching of pencils on paper. Miss Myrtle took only moments to gather them up and count the votes. Everyone watched her every move as she stood up from her desk. "It gives me great pleasure to award Ivan Tippen with the Rainbow Project Award and to declare him Morristown's official weatherman!"

Ivan shook his teacher's hand and accepted the shiny brass statue of a rainbow. He stood before his classmates and the parents. "Thank you, Miss Myrtle. I would like to share this award with my best friend, Jake and his Grandpa Windsor. They definitely helped me with my research!"

Ivan ran to the open window and waved his trophy high in the air. "And a special thank you to Randu and Wazzu!" He turned and faced his beaming parents, "Five down – none to go."

ISBN 1412087988-8